AFRICA

Why Leopard has Spots

Series created by

Claudia Lloyd

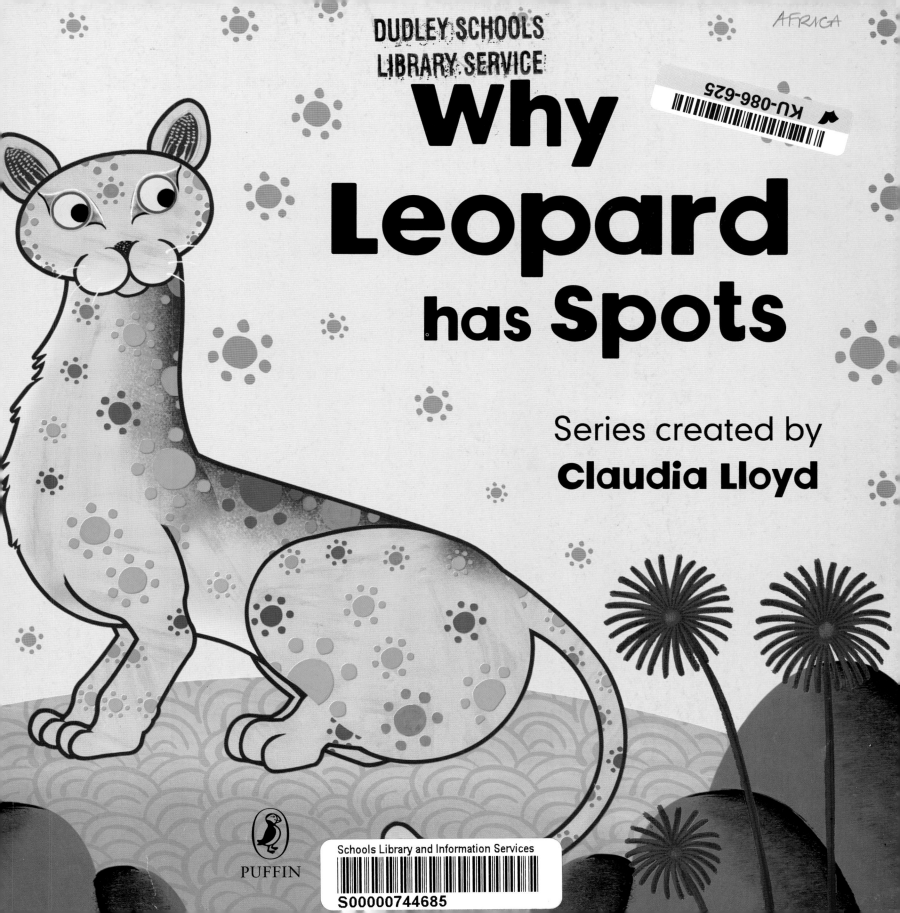

PUFFIN

**Text based on the script
written by Bruce Hobson
and Claudia Lloyd.**

**Illustrations from the TV animation produced
by Tiger Aspect Productions Limited and
Homeboyz Entertainment Kenya.**

PUFFIN BOOKS:
Published by the Penguin Group: London, New York,
Australia, Canada, India, Ireland, New Zealand and South
Africa. Penguin Books Ltd, Registered Offices: 80 Strand, London
WC2R 0RL, England. Published in Puffin Books 2012.

Made and printed in China.

001 – 10 9 8 7 6 5 4 3 2 1

ISBN: 978–0–141–34216–0

You see there was a time
when Leopard **didn't** have spots.
Her coat was as **plain** as **plain** can be
and she was very, very **shy** . . .

"There's **Leopard!**
There she is!"

"**Where?**
Where is she?"

Leopard didn't feel **special** like all the other animals, and she longed for a **beautiful** coat like Mama Cheetah's.

So Leopard **hid** herself away in the long grass.

"How many **spots** have you got?"

"Lots and lots!"

"Do you like my **spots**, Mama?"

"Ah, my cubs!"
said Mama Cheetah.
"When you grow up you're
going to be **beautiful** cats."

Lion saw Leopard hiding in the bush.

"**Jambo**, Leopard," said Lion.
"Come out and say hello.
It's been a while since I **saw** you."

"I **like** it that way, Your Majesty,"
said Leopard. "But I do wish you
a very **good day**."

The Monkeys told all the other animals that they had actually **seen** Leopard.

"But **nobody** ever sees Leopard," said Hippo. "Where was she?"

"Near Mama Cheetah!"

"We must **find** her!"

But they were so busy **looking** for Leopard that they didn't see Puff Adder.

"Oh no!
I've just squished Puff Adder!" said Elephant.
"What do I do **now?**"

"Stay **calm**, everyone,"
said Tortoise. "Now, Elephant,
lift up your **foot.**
Slowly does it . . .
Do just what I say and . . .

"...RUN!"

The animals ran as **fast** as they could because they were afraid of Puff Adder.

"That was **close!**"
said Tickbird.

"Wait for me!"

"Yes, you were **lucky**, Elephant," said Hippo. "Puff Adder could have given you a nasty **bite!**"

"I hope Puff Adder is OK," said Elephant.

Leopard saw **everything** from her hiding place in the long grass.

"Oh dear. I'm **squished** and completely out of **puff!**" said Puff Adder. "Can some animal **help** me?"

"Not **me!**" whispered Tortoise from inside his shell.

"I'll **help** you, Puff Adder," said Leopard.
"If you promise **not** to **bite** me."

"Oh, I promise, Leopard," said Puff Adder.
"I only bite if you **frighten** me
or make me **jump.**"

So Leopard gently picked up Puff Adder
and took him back to her **cave.**

"The others will **never**
believe me!" said Tortoise.

A little time later, Tortoise told the animals what had happened.

"And Puff Adder didn't **bite** Leopard?" said Elephant.

"Not this time he **didn't**," said Tortoise.

"But Puff Adder always **bites**," said Tickbird.

"When Puff Adder feels **better** he will want to **bite**," said Lion. "I must go **immediately** and warn Leopard."

"Me too!" said Monkey. "Can I come? **Please?**"

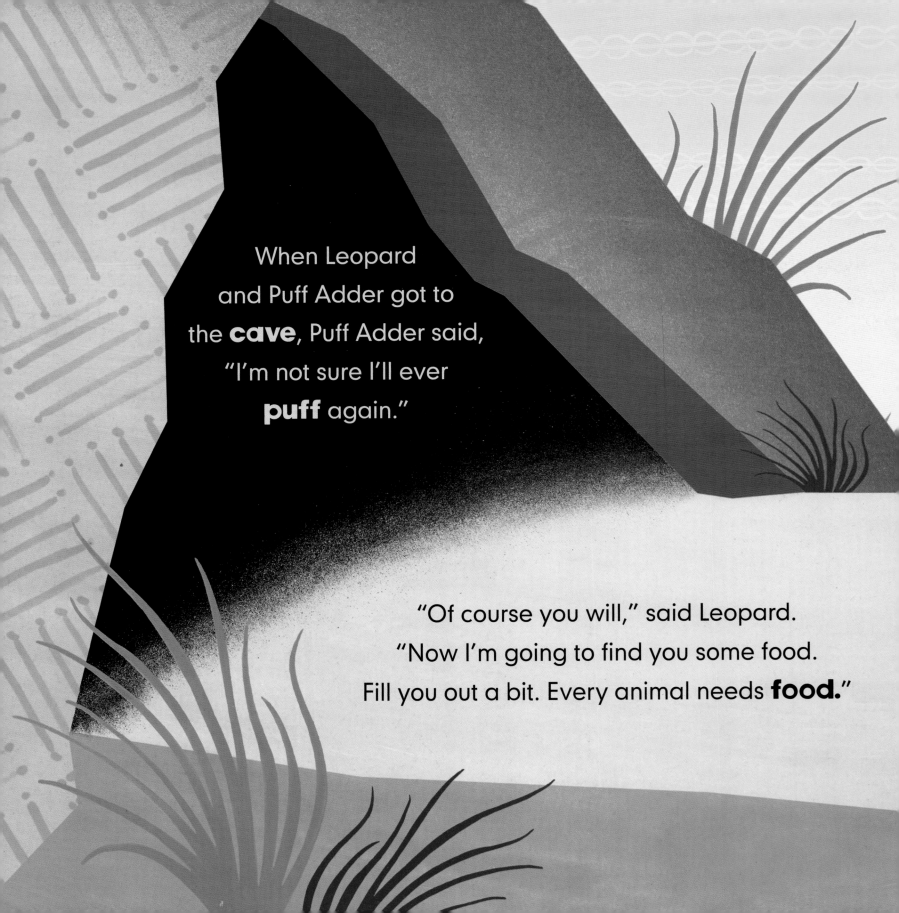

When Leopard
and Puff Adder got to
the **cave**, Puff Adder said,
"I'm not sure I'll ever
puff again."

"Of course you will," said Leopard.
"Now I'm going to find you some food.
Fill you out a bit. Every animal needs **food.**"

"Such **kindness!**" said Puff Adder.
"Thank you, Leopard. **Asante.**"

"Monkey, are you **following** me?" said Lion.

"You know it's too **dangerous.**"

"I thought you might need
some **help** finding Puff Adder,"
said Monkey. "I am **good**
at finding things!"

"Come along then," said Lion.
"But you'd better **stay** close to me."

"But I'm not quite **myself** yet.
There's **one more** thing I have to do . . .

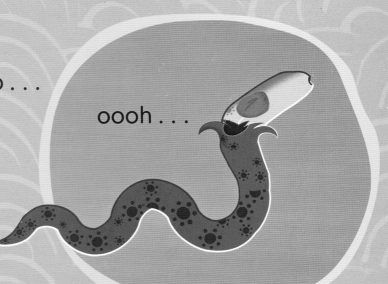

oooh . . .

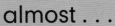

almost . . .

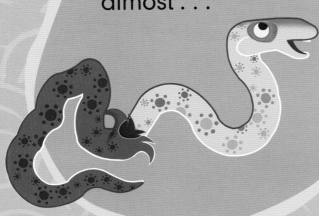

. . . **there!**"

"I've never seen **that**
before!" said Leopard.

"**Shedding my skin?**" said Puff Adder. "It's a special
trick of mine. Now I'm back to my **new** self!"

"Oh, I wish I could have **new** skin and **pretty** colours like you," said Leopard. "My coat is as **plain** as **plain** can be."

"Well, maybe **I** can help **you**," said Puff Adder. "But I'll have to make a tiny **nip** on the end of your tail . . .

Then Puff Adder sang a **Tinga Tinga lullaby** to his new friend Leopard.

"It's time to **sleep**, sleep true, sleep **deep** . . .

Dream nice, dream **long** . . .

I'll sing this **song**, and watch you while you dream **along** . . .

dream of **Tinga** . . . you **belong.**"

And the next morning Leopard woke to find
she had a **beautiful new coat.**

"**Asante, rafiki!**
Thank you, dear friend,"
said Leopard.

"It was my pleasure," said Puff Adder.
"One **kindness** deserves another. And now I want
to wriggle all over **Tinga Tinga.** Goodbye!"

Lion and Monkey had been searching **everywhere** when finally they found Puff Adder's **tracks** in the sand. The tracks came from Leopard's cave.

"Leopard, are you **all right?**" called Lion.

"**Leopard!** You have changed **completely!**" said Lion.

"Look at your beautiful **spots!**" said Monkey.

"Asante, thank you," said Leopard. "It's all down to my **friend** Puff Adder. I **helped** him and he repaid my kindness with this **beautiful** new coat in his colours."

"You **have** to come and show everyone at the waterhole," said Monkey.

"No, Monkey," said Leopard. "You know I like to keep myself to myself. **You** will have to tell the animals."

"But they won't **believe** me," said Monkey.

"They will when you show them Puff Adder's **skin**," said Leopard.

So Monkey told the other animals the **amazing** story.

" . . . And then Puff Adder bit Leopard on the end of her **tail!**" said Monkey. "And now Leopard **looks** like Puff Adder!"

"I don't **believe** it," said Elephant.

"Monkey is telling
the **truth**," said Lion.
"Now Leopard has a
beautiful new coat."

"**Never!**" said Hippo.

So you see, Puff Adder was right,
one kindness does deserve **another.**

And that's why
Leopard has **spots.**